GREAT ILLUSTRATED CLASSICS

IVANHOE

Sir Walter Scott

adapted by
Malvina G. Vogel

Illustrations by
Pablo Marcos Studios

BARONET BOOKS, New York, New York

GREAT ILLUSTRATED CLASSICS

edited by
Joshua E. Hanft

Contents

About the Author

On August 15, 1771, Walter Scott was born in Edinburgh, Scotland. When he was still a baby, Walter contracted a form of polio that left him lame for life. While his brothers and sisters ran about playing, Walter became an avid reader. Although he studied law to please his father, he began writing in his free time and found success with his poems, ballads, and essays.

Years afterward, Walter became intrigued with the idea of writing historical novels. He placed his fictional characters in actual historical events (the Crusades and tournaments at Ashby), alongside actual people in history (King Richard the Lion-Hearted, Prince John, and Robin Hood). While his novels were all very successful, *Ivanhoe* became his most popular.

Strangely enough, no one knew that it was Walter Scott who wrote these novels, for he published them anonymously. Novels were considered a trivial form of literature at that time, and Scott feared risking his reputation as a fine poet and his standing as a court magistrate by putting his name to such works, even though they made him a very rich man. He couldn't know then that he would later be renowned as the originator of the historical novel, a writer who would influence other writers all over the world.

Agonizing stomach problems plagued Scott throughout his life. They created such pain that many of his novels, including *Ivanhoe*, were dictated by him to a servant while he lay in bed, getting up only to act out a scene or some dialogue as he wrote it.

For his great contributions to English literature, he was made a baronet by King George IV and addressed by the title *Sir*.

Sir Walter Scott lived his life by the very same code of chivalry his knights lived by, with truth and honor and courage, until his death in 1832.

Was He Dead or Was He a Prisoner?

CHAPTER 1

Saxon and Norman Enemies

In the year 1192, the people of England feared for the life of their beloved king, Richard I, also called Richard the Lion-Hearted. Was he dead or was he a prisoner somewhere? He had been returning home from his Crusade in the Holy Land when he disappeared. The Crusades were religious wars being fought in Jerusalem by Christians from all over Europe against Turkish invaders.

Rumors reached England accusing Richard's brother, Prince John, of plotting the king's imprisonment in some foreign country so he could rule in his place, which he had been doing during Richard's absence.

Both Richard and John were Plantagenets, the French royal family that was descended from William of Normandy, the king who had conquered England over a hundred years earlier. Even now, many Englishmen, or Saxons as they called themselves, had a fierce hatred for the nobles they called Normans.

On their part, the Normans considered the Saxons beneath them, and they haughtily demanded obedience and respect from them at all times.

In spite of these feelings, many nobles and knights, both Saxon and Norman, had followed Richard on his Crusade. Some had gone because of their Christian beliefs, while others sought military glory or simply had the spirit of adventure.

Two of these knights, both Normans, had recently returned from the Holy Land and were now riding at the head of their party of squires

Two Knights Had Recently Returned.

and guards through Sherwood Forest, near the village of Sheffield. The knights, Brian de Bois-Guilbert and Maurice de Bracy, were on their way to the town of Ashby, where a tournament to show off their knightly skills was to be held in a few days.

This was not the safest of roads for the horsemen, even with their guards, since a gallant band of outlaws, led by the notorious Robin of Locksley and his Merry Men, roamed this forest, robbing even the bravest travelers. Now, with Ashby still a day's ride away and a storm approaching quickly, the travelers needed to find a place to spend the night.

Nearing a fork in the road, the riders overtook a lone man dressed in a long, black hooded cloak and carrying a tall staff. The cross of palm leaves attached to the staff identified him as a Palmer, a religious pilgrim recently returned from the Holy Land.

Bois-Guilbert called out, "You there, do you know a nobleman's castle nearby where we can

A Lone Man in a Long, Black-hooded Cloak

be fed and lodged overnight with proper hospitality due our positions and titles?"

"Certainly, my Lord," replied the Palmer. "The castle of Rotherwood, home of Cedric the Saxon, is near. I'm headed there myself and will gladly show you the way."

"Cedric?" mumbled De Bracy. "That wealthy Saxon nobleman hates all of us. He surely won't welcome Normans at his castle."

"We're not *asking* for his hospitality," sneered Bois-Guilbert arrogantly. "Normans have a right to *demand* it of any Saxon."

"But we wouldn't want to arouse Cedric's anger, especially in front of his beautiful daughter, Lady Rowena," cautioned De Bracy.

"My Lords," interrupted the Palmer, "Lady Rowena is not Cedric's daughter. She's a princess, a distant relative whom he raised. But she's as dear to him as if she *were* his daughter. If she were offended in any way, Cedric wouldn't think twice about sending you or any knight from his house."

"We're Not *Asking* for His Hospitality."

"So I've heard," added De Bracy. "People say he is so fierce and so protective of her that he even banished his own son, Ivanhoe, from his home because the young man fell in love with her. Cedric insists on someone of royal blood—a prince, at least—as her husband. I also heard that he disinherited his son for going on the Crusade with the king."

"This is certainly one man whose anger we don't want to provoke," said Bois-Guilbert. "We must be certain to show him the utmost respect and politeness at Rotherwood."

As the Palmer led the travelers deep into the woods, he seemed to know every twist and turn of the path that led to Rotherwood. And well he should, for he had lived there all his life.

But as familiar as the Palmer was with these woods, even he couldn't detect the band of Merry Men hiding on either side of the path, waiting for the signal from their leader, Robin of Locksley, to attack and rob the travelers.

The Band of Merry Men

But that signal never came. The only sound was a gasp, as Robin whispered to his friend and advisor, Friar Tuck, "Good Lord! That's Ivanhoe at the front of that group of travelers! He must have just returned from the Crusades. At least *he* hasn't met the dreadful fate that our beloved King Richard did!"

"That's true," said the Friar. "But why is he dressed as a Palmer? Why is he leading those Norman knights to his father's castle? To a man who considers him dead? Has he now turned traitor and sided with the Normans?"

"I think not, good Tuck," said Robin. "Ivanhoe is too loyal a Saxon and too brave a knight to ever turn against his people. I'm certain he's planning something, and I'm just as certain that we'll find out what it is before many days pass!"

"Good Lord! That's Ivanhoe!"

The Home of Cedric the Saxon

CHAPTER 2

Visitors to Rotherwood

When Ivanhoe led the Normans out of the woods, he pointed ahead to a cluster of low stone buildings surrounded by a moat and a tall stockade fence. "That is Rotherwood," he said, "the home of Cedric the Saxon."

Once the travelers identified themselves, the drawbridge was lowered and the Normans and their party entered the courtyard.

A servant showed them into a huge hall, where a long table in the shape of a "T" was set for the evening meal. Across the top, the table was raised on a carpeted dais a step above the long, lower end.

Cedric the Saxon sat in a large, carved chair at the center of the dais table, with the Lady Rowena seated on his right. He was anxious to start his evening meal when a servant appeared at the door and announced, "My Lord, the good knights Brian de Bois-Guilbert and Maurice de Bracy, with their squires and guards, request your hospitality and lodging for the night."

"Normans!" Cedric muttered to Rowena in disgust. "Even though Bois-Guilbert has proven himself a brave and fearless knight in the Holy Land and he *is* a Knight Templar who has taken all the vows of chivalry plus those that prohibit him from marrying, I know him to be a cruel, arrogant man. And as for that De Bracy, why he's only a puppet doing Prince John's bidding. Still, it is only for one night and I cannot deny my hospitality to anyone, Saxon or Norman." Then aloud, he replied to his servant, "Invite them to enter and join us

"Normans!" Cedric Muttered in Disgust.

at dinner. They are welcome at Rotherwood."

The two knights entered the hall and approached the dais, while their attendants and the Palmer seated themselves at the foot of the long, lower table with the servants.

Cedric rose to greet his guests and, with a wave of his hand, motioned them to the two carved dais seats at his left.

As he took his seat, Maurice de Bracy was so captivated by the beautiful princess Rowena that he couldn't tear his eyes away from her face. But Rowena didn't care for such admiring looks from a Norman and she glared at De Bracy until he lowered his eyes.

Cedric caught these looks and reminded De Bracy, "Sir Knight, a Saxon princess does not welcome the attentions of Norman knights and Templars whose ancestors took away her lands and murdered her sub—"

Bois-Guilbert angrily interrupted his host. "We have been fighting and dying in the Holy Land in England's name. Surely we can pay a

Captivated by the Beautiful Princess Rowena

compliment to an English lady."

De Bracy tried to soften the Templar's angry words. "Sir Cedric, I meant no offense to the Lady Rowena, and I ask her pardon for staring at her, but never have I seen such beauty anywhere! May I apologize by offering to escort you both along these dangerous roads to the tournament at Ashby?"

"I have no need for an escort to travel in my own land!" snapped Cedric indignantly. "And I don't know if we're even going to the tournament. To me, it's nothing more than a Norman game of showing off and practicing for war."

"I accept your apology, Sir Knight," Rowena told De Bracy. "But rather than give me compliments, give me news of the war in the Holy Land." What she wanted to hear most was news of Ivanhoe, but she couldn't come right out and ask for such news because no one at Rotherwood was allowed to mention his name.

But before either knight could give Rowena any news, a servant entered the hall to an-

"I Have No Need for an Escort!"

nounce that a stranger was at the gate begging for hospitality for the night.

"Bring him in, whoever he is," ordered Cedric. "With this storm raging, no one deserves to spend the night outdoors."

A few minutes later, a tall, thin old man appeared at the door to the hall. "I am Isaac of York," he stated, bowing to Cedric and removing his high, square cap.

The master of Rotherwood invited Isaac to join them at dinner by waving him to a place at the lower end of the table. But none of the servants or guests made room for the old man because he was a Jew.

Only the Palmer rose from his place. "Sit here by the fire, old man," he said. "My clothes have dried and I have eaten. Yours are still soaked and you need food as well."

With that, the Palmer walked towards the dais. Bois-Guilbert was busy praising the superior fighting abilities of his Templars when Rowena interrupted him.

"I am Isaac of York."

"But your knights weren't able to win back Jerusalem, were they?" she taunted. "And the Templars weren't there alone. Weren't King Richard's gallant knights with him as well?"

"They were only second best," sneered the Templar scornfully.

"They were second to NONE!" mocked a voice nearby.

Everyone turned to where the Palmer was standing, his face still hidden by the hood of his cloak. "I repeat, Richard's men were second to none! Think back, Bois-Guilbert, to a tournament held at Acre during a break in the war. King Richard and five of his Saxon knights competed against six of your Norman knights, including De Bracy and yourself. Do you remember how that turned out?"

While De Bracy hung his head in embarrassment, Bois-Guilbert scowled with rage. He reached for his sword, then realized that this was not the place to start a fight.

Cedric, however, was delighted to learn of a

"Richard's Men Were Second to None!"

Saxon victory, and he said, "Tell me, good Palmer, who were those noble Saxon knights?"

"Gladly, my Lord." And the Palmer named five of the combatants.

"Yes, yes, and who was the sixth?" shouted Cedric eagerly.

"A young knight who's not very well known. I don't remember his name."

"I doubt that your memory has suddenly failed you, Sir Palmer," said the Templar. "I'll tell you who that knight was, Lord Cedric, for in spite of his youth, he was renowned for his ability in battle, and he defeated me only because my horse fell. If he were in England at this moment, in fact at the tournament at Ashby this week, I'd gladly challenge Ivanhoe to a combat again."

Cedric gasped, but didn't utter a word.

"Yes, I do recall now," said the Palmer softly. "His name *was* Ivanhoe. The young knight was wounded in battle and stayed behind to convalesce when Richard left. But he fell into

"I'd Gladly Challenge Ivanhoe Again!"

the hands of some of your Norman friends, Sir Templar, and they didn't treat him too well. I imagine he's recovered by now and on the way home. When he arrives, I'm certain he'll accept your challenge."

"And if he refuses," warned Bois-Guilbert, "I'll proclaim him a coward throughout all of Europe!"

"That will never be necessary!" shouted Rowena, jumping up angrily. "I've known Ivanhoe since we were children, and I add my own guarantee to that of this holy Palmer. If Ivanhoe hadn't been wounded and were here now, he'd be the first to defend the honor of Saxon England at Ashby."

Cedric now broke his silence. "Sir Templar, if you need further assurance of the honor of a true Saxon, I give you mine. The honor of Cedric stands behind the honor of his son, Ivanhoe!"

"That Will Never Be Necessary!"

"Seize Him and Hold Him for Ransom."

CHAPTER 3

Rescuing Isaac from Danger

After dinner, Cedric ordered his servants to lead his guests to their chambers for the night. As the travelers were leaving the dining hall, the Palmer overheard Brian de Bois-Guilbert whispering orders to his men.

"When Isaac of York leaves in the morning, follow him. As soon as he is out of sight of Rotherwood, seize him and take him to the castle of Reginald Front-de-Boeuf. We'll rob Isaac of the money he carries and hold him for ransom as well. His friends will pay well for his release."

The Palmer pretended not to have heard anything as he was escorted by Cedric's long-time family servant, Gurth, along a dark stone passageway in the servants' part of the castle. Ahead of them, they saw Isaac being led into one room, and beyond that was the door which Gurth opened for the Palmer. The Palmer lay down fully dressed on a crude straw bed. When he was certain that Gurth and the other servants had all retired to their own rooms, he tiptoed out of his and silently entered Isaac's.

The old man was moaning and tossing uneasily in his sleep when the Palmer nudged him with his staff. Isaac's eyes flew open in a panic.

"Don't be afraid of me, Isaac. I'm your friend," whispered the Palmer. "I've come to warn you that Bois-Guilbert's men will seize you when you leave in the morning. You must leave tonight if you want to avoid danger."

The old man tried to rise up from his bed, but he fell to his knees in terror and began to weep.

"Don't Be Afraid! I'm Your Friend."

"There's no time for weeping. We must leave Rotherwood immediately while everyone is asleep. I know every path in this forest and I'll lead you to safety."

Isaac, however, was suspicious. "Don't betray me, Palmer. I'm only a poor merchant."

"Why would I do such a thing? Even if you were rich, I have no need of money. I'm a Palmer who has taken the vows of poverty."

"Then I thank you, good Palmer," said Isaac with a sigh of relief. "But so many of your English nobles persecute my people when we lend them money, which they use only to support their extravagant lifestyles. Then they refuse to pay it back and threaten us. We're always in danger. Why, even Prince John himself, does this. And almost every nobleman follows his lead. So please try to understand why I was suspicious. But I do believe you. Let us hurry and leave."

"I must first find someone I can trust to unlock the gate for us." And the Palmer hurried

"We Must Leave Rotherwood Immediately."

out the door and crossed the hallway into Gurth's room.

"Wake up, Gurth," he ordered. "I need you to unlock the rear gate and let down the drawbridge. Isaac and I wish to leave."

"No one leaves until the gate is opened in the morning," mumbled Gurth, turning over to go back to sleep.

The Palmer then leaned over the bed and whispered something in the servant's ear. Gurth immediately jumped up and nervously pulled on his shirt and pants. He bowed to the Palmer, then rushed out the door.

Isaac, who had been watching at the door, was puzzled at the sudden change in Gurth's behavior. But he followed the Palmer as he hurried behind Gurth into the passageway.

As the three headed out of the building, the Palmer ordered Gurth, "Bring Isaac's mule to the other side of the moat and borrow one from Cedric's stables for me."

Gurth ran to the stables and several min-

The Palmer Hurried Behind Gurth.

utes later met the two men with the mules outside the castle walls. After Isaac and the
Palmer had mounted their mules, the Palmer
reached down to shake Gurth's hand. But the
servant drew the hand up to his lips and
kissed it respectfully.

"God be with you," he whispered. "I promise
to join you at Ashby as soon as I can, my Lord.
And I thank you for naming me your squire. I
pledge my loyalty in serving you."

Isaac and the Palmer rode in silence for
many hours until they reached the edge of the
town of Sheffield. As the road forked, they
drew their mules to a halt.

"Please come with me to my friend Zareth,"
said Isaac. "He's a wealthy man and will most
certainly help me repay your kindness."

"I don't need any payment or any reward,"
insisted the Palmer.

"But I know there *is* something you do need.
A horse and armor, perhaps?"

The Palmer jerked up his head, startled.

They Rode in Silence.

"How did you guess that? After all, you see me dressed as a holy man and holy men don't have a need for armor."

"Forgive me," said Isaac, smiling. "But your words of warning last night were not those of a holy man, and when you bent over my bed, I saw a knight's chain under your robe. But that's not important now. I have a friend in Sheffield who sells the finest horses and weapons in England. You will pick out what you need, and when the tournament is over, you can return them or pay him."

"But surely you know that if I lose in the tournament, my horse and armor and weapons will be forfeited to the winning knight."

"In my heart I know you will *not* lose, my son. Besides, I don't care about forfeiting a horse or armor or some weapons. But I *do* care about you losing a limb or your life."

"Thank you, Isaac. Let us be off."

"I Know You Will *Not* Lose"

The Tournament at Ashby

CHAPTER 4

The Tournament at Ashby

Even though the lower classes of Englishmen lived under the poorest conditions and suffered from a lack of food, neither poverty nor work nor illness stopped the masses from attending a tournament. Great distances didn't keep nobles or knights away either.

The tournament at Ashby was certain to be even more spectacular than others because the most famous knights in the land were facing each other and because Prince John was to be there to crown the Champion.

The field on which the tournament was to

take place was a beautiful grassy meadow, a quarter-mile long and surrounded by wooded slopes on all sides. A palisade—a fence of pointed wooden stakes—enclosed the field of combat, with openings at the northern and southern ends through which the combatants would enter and face each other.

Outside the openings at the southern end, five magnificent pavilions, or tents, had been set up, each in colors matching those of the knight occupying it. In front of each pavilion hung the knight's shield, guarded diligently by his loyal squire. The center pavilion, the pavilion of honor, had been assigned to Brian de Bois-Guilbert, who was considered the Champion of all the knights.

At the northern end, pavilions had been set up for the challengers, along with those for servants and refreshment sellers.

On the eastern and western sides, galleries had been erected and covered with carpets. Here, knights, nobles, town officials, all with

Pavilions for the Challengers

their ladies, would be seated from the center to the end, according to their rank and wealth. The poor masses, however, used the slopes of the surrounding hills and branches of the trees from which to view the tournament.

One gallery at the center of the eastern side stood higher than those alongside it. A richly decorated canopy with the royal coat of arms covered a raised throne on which Prince John was seated. Perched on his hand was his pet falcon. John's handsome but haughty face turned from side to side as he boldly eyed the ladies in the galleries, knowing that the one selected as Queen of Beauty and Love would soon be seated on the flowered throne beside him.

John's eyes stopped on a beautiful, dark-haired young woman clinging to the arm of Isaac of York as they made their way to their seats a distance away from the prince. The woman's diamond necklace and rich silk gown had already attracted the attention and envy

He Boldly Eyed the Ladies in the Gallery.

of many ladies in the gallery.

"Isaac of York, my friend and banker!" called Prince John, mocking the old man from whom he often borrowed money. "Who is that lovely lady on your arm?"

"This is my daughter Rebecca, Your Grace," answered Isaac with a low bow.

"Her beauty requires that she sit closer to the royal gallery. Bring her here." And John turned to the noble family in the gallery beside his and ordered, "Cedric, my Saxon lord, move over and make room for Isaac and his daughter."

When Cedric chose to ignore the prince's order, Maurice de Bracy, seated beside John, jumped up and reached his lance out toward Cedric. But the Lord of Rotherwood was even quicker with his sword and, with a single blow, cut off the knight's lance at its tip.

"Good shot!" called a distant voice from a nearby tree branch.

"Good shot! Good shot!" repeated a chorus of

"Good Shot!"

voices from tree branches around him.

Prince John looked in the direction of the voices, his face red with rage. The yeoman, or commoner, who had first called out, was dressed in Lincoln-green and carried a six-foot-long bow in his hand. The men in trees around him were dressed in the same green, except for a rather stout friar in a brown robe. All were cheering the yeoman on.

"That's tellin' 'em, Robin!"

"We'll take Cedric's sword over De Bracy's lance anytime, won't we, Robin?"

At that moment, Waldemar Fitzurse, the prince's chief advisor, whispered in John's ear, "Stay calm, Your Highness. If you answer these yeomen in anger, their cheering will spread to the rest of the crowd and make you look ridiculous. I know these yeomen. They're a band from Sherwood Forest who are loyal to your brother Richard. They'd like nothing better than to embarrass you in front of this huge crowd and ruin this day."

"That's Tellin' 'em, Robin!"

Sulking as he nodded in agreement, Prince John then gave the order for the herald to announce the rules of the tournament.

The trumpets sounded and the crowd became silent. The herald rode to the center of the lists, the field of combat, and began to read from a scroll.

"First, the five knights in this tournament agree to accept all challengers.

"Second, a challenger shall choose any knight as his opponent by touching that knight's shield with his lance. A touch with the *blunt end* of the lance means a courtesy match in which the winner only needs to break his opponent's lance. A touch with the *point* of the lance is the challenge for a fight to the death.

"Third, the knight who breaks five lances today will be named Champion for the day and will crown his choice for Queen of Beauty and Love for the rest of the tournament."

The tournament began, and for the first four sets, Bois-Guilbert, De Bracy, Front-de-Boeuf,

The Trumpets Sounded.

and two other Norman knights easily defeated their Saxon challengers in courtesy matches. The spectators, most of whom were Saxons, were disappointed, but no Saxon felt this disappointment as strongly as Cedric.

"This day is going badly for England," he said to Lady Rowena. "Isn't there anyone to defend the honor of our country? Isn't there anyone to defeat those Normans, especially that arrogant Templar, Bois-Guilbert, and keep him from being crowned champion?"

As if in answer to his question, a single trumpet blare sounded from the northern end of the lists to announce a new challenger. All eyes turned north. A knight, in a suit of steel armor inlaid with gold, rode in through the gate astride a fine-looking white horse. His shield's symbol pictured a young oak tree pulled out of the ground by its roots. Across the shield was etched the word "Disinherited."

As the knight rode through the lists, he saluted Prince John by lowering his lance.

On the Shield Was Etched "Disinherited."

Something about the way he carried himself seemed to please the crowd, and they soon began calling out the names of the knights each wanted him to challenge.

But the Disinherited Knight had obviously made up his mind in advance, for he rode directly to the pavilions of four knights and touched each one's shield with the blunt end of his sword. Then he rode to the center pavilion and reined his horse to a halt. He raised his lance and struck the shield of Brian de Bois-Guilbert with its point.

The crowd gasped in disbelief! Brian de Bois-Guilbert, himself, gasped in disbelief! The Disinherited Knight was challenging him to a fight to the death!

But the Templar immediately regained his composure and haughtily demanded, "You had better have gone to church this morning to confess your sins, Sir Knight, for you are about to die, if not at the hands of my fellow Normans, then surely at mine!"

The Crowd Gasped in Disbelief!

"I think not, Bois-Guilbert, and I would suggest that you take a fresh horse and lance for yourself, for you will need both when you face me!" With that, the Disinherited Knight dug his spurs into his horse's sides and galloped to the northern end of the lists to await the call to combat.

Bois-Guilbert returned to the southern end, where he took the advice of his challenger. He ordered a rested, vigorous horse, a stronger lance, and a thicker shield. Then he stood in front of his pavilion to watch the Disinherited Knight take on De Bracy, Front-de-Boeuf, and two other Normans, one after the other. On his first pass against them, he easily unseated each knight.

As the defeated De Bracy returned to his pavilion, Bois-Guilbert came up to him and said, "I've been watching that knight very closely, and there's something strangely familiar about his style. I almost get the feeling I've seen him fight before. Maybe I've even fought

He Easily Unseated Each Knight.

him myself."

"We'll know soon enough," said De Bracy. "He'll have to remove his visor and helmet at the end of the tournament."

It was now Bois-Guilbert's turn to face his challenger. As he took his position at the southern end of the lists, a hush fell over the spectators. Most were on the side of the courageous Disinherited Knight, but feared he was now doomed to death.

At Prince John's signal, the trumpets blared and the knights sped towards each other. Lances were thrust at shields, sending shocks through both men. Their horses recoiled backwards, but recovered their balance. The knights turned and rode away, each to his own end of the lists, amid shouts and applause from the spectators.

Once the two were in position, the crowd became silent again. The trumpets blared to signal the second charge, and the knights galloped towards each other.

The Knights Sped Toward Each Other.

The Templar struck first, his lance crashing into the Disinherited Knight's shield with such force that the wooden pole shattered to pieces. But at that exact moment, the Disinherited Knight thrust his lance into the Templar's visor, where its point stuck in the bars.

As Bois-Guilbert tried to keep his balance, the strap on his saddle broke, throwing him to the ground. In a rage because of his disgrace and the jeers of the crowd, he got to his feet and drew his sword.

The Disinherited Knight jumped down from his horse with his own sword drawn. The rules of the tournament, however, did not permit the two to continue their combat on foot, and the officials separated them before their swords could strike a blow.

"You may be Champion today, Sir Knight, but we'll meet again," swore Brian de Bois-Guilbert. "And then no one will separate us."

"I'll be ready to meet you any time and with

"We'll Meet Again!"

any weapon. And it will be a fight to the death!"

The officials then asked the new Champion to raise his visor when he faced the prince, but he refused very courteously. Since the laws of chivalry permitted any knight to enter a tournament disguised, Prince John could not insist that the Champion unmask.

John was angry that his favorite Norman knights had been defeated, and he stormed at Fitzurse, "I cannot believe that there's a knight in England capable of defeating five of my finest knights and we haven't heard of him. Do you have any idea who he is?"

"None at all, Your Highness, unless he's a knight who went with King Richard to the Holy Land and has now returned home. Perhaps it's even the king himself!"

Prince John turned pale as death. "Heaven forbid!" he gasped and he shrank down on his throne. "Fitzurse, stand by me and protect me. See to it that my knights do the same."

Prince John Turned Pale as Death.

"Your Highness, you are in no danger. This Champion before you is not as tall or as broad as your brother. Look at him and see."

John nodded nervously, then made a speech praising the Champion, as was the custom. He waited for a reply from the Knight, but all he received as his thanks was a deep bow.

Continuing on with the ceremonies, Prince John announced, "Sir Disinherited Knight, it is now your duty to name the fair lady of your choice to be Queen of Beauty and Love." And he placed a crown of gold hearts on the tip of the Knight's lance.

The Disinherited Knight rode along the galleries and didn't stop until he was in front of Lady Rowena. Cedric's smile, which had been on his face since the mysterious stranger defeated the five Normans, now widened as he realized that a Saxon lady was to be crowned Queen.

A cheer went up from the crowd as the Champion tilted his lance towards Rowena, so

A Cheer Went Up from the Crowd.

that the crown could slide into her hands.

"Long live Lady Rowena! Long live the Saxon princess!" chanted the crowd.

Although these cheers infuriated Prince John and his advisors, they knew that the rules of chivalry—rules the Normans, themselves, had made years ago—required them to accept the choice made by the Champion. So, John left his throne and made his way to the gallery where Rowena and Cedric were seated.

He took the golden crown from her hands and placed it on her head. "Let this crown be the symbol of your choice as Queen at this tournament. I invite you and your noble father to be my guests tonight at a banquet at Ashby Castle."

Cedric would never consider dining with the king he hated, but for Rowena's sake he declined the invitation with politeness.

John then turned to the Disinherited Knight and said, "Surely *you* will celebrate your victory at the banquet with me?"

"Long Live Lady Rowena!"

"I regret, My Prince, that I cannot. I'm very tired from today's tournament and I must rest for tomorrow's combat."

Prince John was not accustomed to having his invitations refused, and as he turned to leave, his voice dripped with sarcasm. "Then we will just have to force ourselves to dine without our Queen or Champion!"

Waldemar Fitzurse turned away, muttering to himself, "This foolish behavior will turn the people against the prince. But I can't control every word he speaks, and I dare not criticize him if I want to protect my position at court and my head as well."

So Fitzurse shrugged his shoulders and followed Prince John out of the gallery.

The first tournament day was ended.

"Without Our Queen or Champion!"

He Found Gurth Waiting.

CHAPTER 5

A Debt Is Repaid

When the Disinherited Knight returned to his pavilion, he found Gurth waiting. After serving dinner to his master, the young squire announced, "My Lord, the five squires belonging to the knights you defeated today are outside, each with his master's horse and weapons and armor."

"Yes, Gurth. According to the laws of chivalry, I have the right to keep their battle gear or demand payment if I return them. I'll see these squires in a moment, as soon as I cover my face with the hood on my robe. I don't want to be recognized."

Once that was done, the Disinherited Knight stepped outside. To four of the squires, he explained, "Sirs, please tell your masters that I commend them on their bravery in the tournament. I don't want their horses or weapons or armor, but I do want payment, since I must pay for all the equipment I used in the tournament."

"Each of our masters offers you fifty gold coins," said Front-de-Boeuf's squire, speaking for all five.

"I thank you and accept it from four of your masters," said the Disinherited Knight. Then turning to the fifth man, Bois-Guilbert's squire, he said, "Tell your master that I refuse any payment from him. My fight with him is not over. When we next meet in the lists, I will fight him to the death!"

When the Disinherited Knight went back into his pavilion, he handed Gurth ten gold coins. "I know the risk you took leaving my

"I Refuse Any Payment."

father and coming to serve me, loyal Gurth, so we must both keep our identities secret. Now I need you to ride into Ashby and find Isaac. Give him this bag of gold to pay his friend for my horse and armor and weapons."

Within the hour, Gurth had found Isaac and Rebecca staying at the home of their friend. The squire was admitted into the house and shown into Isaac and Rebecca's apartment. After explaining why he had come, he counted out the eighty coins the old man asked for.

"Your master is a fine young man," Isaac told Gurth. "I was just telling my daughter that very thing, wasn't I, Rebec— Now, where has my daughter gone?" Then turning back to Gurth, Isaac continued, "Tell your master that Rebecca and I wish him well in the tournament tomorrow."

As Gurth was about to leave the darkened house, Rebecca came out of a room near the front door. "Good squire," she whispered, "please come in here for a moment."

"Come Here for a Moment!"

Gurth followed Rebecca into the room. The young woman whispered, "How much money did my father ask your master to pay?"

"Eighty gold coins, my lady."

"My father was jesting with you, good man. He owes your master much more than these pieces of gold could ever repay." Then she handed Gurth a purse and continued. "You will find one hundred gold coins here. Return eighty to your master and keep the other twenty for yourself. Oh, and don't waste time thanking me. Just hurry back to your master and be careful traveling through this crowded town at this late hour."

Gurth thanked Rebecca and hurriedly left the house. Once he was out on the dark street, he whispered to himself, "She's an angel from heaven! Twenty pieces of gold from her, added to the ten from my brave master! Soon I'll be able to buy my freedom and truly be a squire to my young lord without hiding my face or my name from anyone."

"Twenty Pieces of Gold."

Each Would Choose a Side.

CHAPTER 6

The Mysterious Black Knight

The crowd began to gather in the galleries early the next morning, eager to get a good seat for the second day of the tournament. Today would have one hundred knights, all fighting at the same time. Each would choose a side, either the side of the Disinherited Knight—the Champion of the previous day, or the side of Bois-Guilbert—the Champion supported by Prince John.

Once all the spectators were seated, the trumpets announced the arrival of Prince John, escorting Lady Rowena to her Queen's throne beside him.

The knights lined up facing each other at opposite ends of the lists as the herald announced the weapons and rules of that day's combat. He finished by stating, "The battle will come to an end when Prince John decides that too much blood has been spilled and he throws down his staff."

The trumpets sounded once again, and the knights galloped towards each other, meeting in the middle with a deafening crash.

The dust raised by a hundred horses made it impossible for the crowd to view the battle. But when the dust cleared, half the knights could be seen off their horses, fighting hand to hand, while many others lay wounded or dead in the dirt.

Of those still astride their horses, many had tossed away their broken lances and were now fighting with swords and battle-axes. From one moment to the next, one side or the other seemed to be winning. Blows and shouts

Dust Raised by a Hundred Horses!

almost drowned out the moans of the wounded as they were trampled under the feet of maddened horses. This was no longer a courteous display of chivalry among knights; this was only blood and terror and death!

The crowd cheered loudly with each blow, and even the ladies clapped their hands and waved their veils to encourage the knights.

"Fight on, brave knights!" urged Prince John. "Death is better than defeat!"

As the battle continued, the Disinherited Knight and Bois-Guilbert tried to find each other in the crush and confusion of men and horses. But lesser opponents, eager to face a Champion, kept them apart until only a few knights were left.

The two Champions were striking at each other with their swords, much to the delight and admiration of the crowd. Then Maurice de Bracy and Reginald Front-de-Boeuf defeated their opponents at the same moment and immediately charged in from opposite sides to

"Fight on, Brave Knights!"

join the attack on the Disinherited Knight.

Seeing this unfair and unexpected behavior, the crowd let out a warning cry. "Take care, Sir Disinherited! Look to the side!"

Suddenly aware of this new danger, the Disinherited Knight struck a full blow at Bois-Guilbert, then reined back his horse to escape the two knights bearing down on him. They were galloping at such speed that they almost smashed into each other. But at the last minute, they wheeled around and, along with Bois-Guilbert, lunged at the Disinherited Knight with their weapons.

The bravery and skill of the Disinherited Knight in turning and wheeling and striking at one, then the other, permitted him to hold off his opponents. While the crowd continued to applaud his skill, they feared he was doomed to defeat and death unless Prince John stopped this unfair battle.

The crowd started protesting. Even his advisors appealed to him. But John refused to

"Look to the Side!"

throw down his staff. "I will not stop the combat!" he snapped. "This arrogant fellow has chosen to hide his name and his face, in addition to insulting me by refusing my hospitality. He may have won the prize in the name of the Saxons yesterday; however, today it's the Normans' turn to—"

But Prince John was suddenly interrupted by a gasp from the crowd. All eyes turned to a tall, powerfully built knight speeding into the lists on a huge black horse. He was covered from head to toe with black armor, and his hand held a large black shield.

At that moment, the Disinherited Knight was fighting off blows from Bois-Guilbert's sword, with Front de Boeuf's battle-axe ready to come down on his head. But the Black Knight reached them in time to swing his sword at Front-de-Boeuf and fling him off his horse. He then turned to De Bracy and wrenched the Norman's mace from his hand. He swung it over his head and brought it down

From Head to Toe with Black Armor

on De Bracy, knocking him into the dirt, stunned.

With the fight even once again, the Black Knight galloped off the field as the crowd cheered. Then they turned their attention back to the two remaining combatants.

Bois-Guilbert's horse had been wounded and now fell to the ground. With his foot tangled in the stirrup, the Templar lay on the field, helpless, as the Disinherited Knight stood over him.

"Give up and admit defeat!" he cried, waving his sword at the Templar.

Seeing his Champion knight about to be disgraced, Prince John threw down his staff to save Bois-Guilbert and himself that embarrassment. The combat was over.

Chivalry then required Prince John to name the outstanding fighter of the day. "I name the Black Knight," he announced.

"But Your Highness," said Fitzurse, "the victory today was won by the Disinherited

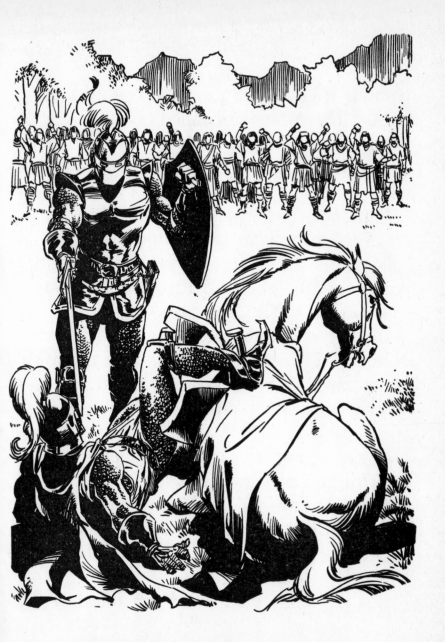

"Give Up and Admit Defeat!"

Knight. He defeated the most challengers."

But John was determined not to honor the Disinherited Knight in any way. "Bring the Black Knight before me," he ordered his marshal.

"I cannot, Your Highness. He's gone. He left after defeating your two knights."

John had no choice. He reluctantly said, "I name the Disinherited Knight Champion of this combat. Bring him here."

Once the Knight stood before him, John announced, "I proclaim you the winner of this tournament. Prepare to receive your crown of victory from the hands of the Queen of Beauty and Love."

Rowena stepped down from her throne as the Knight knelt unsteadily at her feet.

"His head must be uncovered in order to be crowned Champion," the marshal ordered.

"No, no," came a weak voice from inside the Knight's helmet.

But the marshal insisted on following the

"His Head Must be Uncovered."

proper rules, and he slowly and carefully removed the Champion's helmet. A head of short, blond hair framed the pale, bloody face of a handsome young man of twenty-five.

Rowena gasped as she recognized the face of the man she loved. But she quickly forced herself to continue the ceremonies so as not to reveal his identity to the prince.

Placing the crown on the wounded man's drooping head, she proclaimed, "I name you Champion of this tournament, and never was a man more worthy of it than you, Sir Knight."

The Knight pressed her hand to his lips, then he fell, unconscious, at her feet.

Confusion spread among the spectators. But for Cedric, the sudden appearance of his disinherited son came as a complete shock. He rushed to Rowena's side in time to see the marshal removing his son's armor.

"Good grief!" he cried as he held Rowena. "The tip of a lance has broken off and is embedded in Ivanhoe's side!"

"I Name You Champion of this Tournament."

Carrying Him off the Field.

CHAPTER 7

A Warning for Prince John

"Ivanhoe!" Prince John cried to Fitzurse. "He's my brother's loyal Saxon follower. This can only mean trouble for me."

"I don't think so, Your Highness. See how seriously wounded he is. His friends are already carrying him off the field."

"And the Lady Rowena, where has she gone?" demanded Prince John, seeing the empty chair beside him.

"I suppose she's gone to grieve for the wounded knight she loves," sneered De Bracy.

"I have other plans for that wealthy Saxon

beauty," said the prince with a cruel laugh. "I'll make her the bride of a loyal Norman, like you, De Bracy. What do you think about having such a rich and beautiful wife?"

"I'd be grateful till my dying day, Your Highness." And De Bracy bowed deeply.

Any further conversation about Rowena was interrupted at that moment by a guard who approached Prince John and handed him a letter. "This was delivered by a messenger from France, Your Highness."

"F-France?" the prince gasped to Fitzurse. "The country where Richard is imprisoned!" His hands trembled as he unfolded the paper, and his face turned deathly pale at the words: BE WARNED! THE KING HAS ESCAPED!

"We must end the tournament immediately!" John shrieked. "I must flee for my life!"

"Stay calm," said Fitzurse. "Your people mustn't suspect that anything is wrong. We'll say that you've been called away on urgent matters of state and must cancel the events

"I Must Flee for My Life."

scheduled for tomorrow."

"That won't do any good!" cried Prince John, pacing in the gallery. "My people have heard the roar of the lion, the roar of Richard the Lion-Hearted, shaking the woods. Nothing will give my nobles the courage to stand by me."

"If only he had a little courage himself," Fitzurse whispered to De Bracy. "But the moment he hears his brother's name, he changes from a strong, insolent tyrant to a shameless, pitiful weakling."

"Then it's up to us to keep his subjects loyal," replied De Bracy. "Promises of favors and gifts of gold should do that. And we must see to it that John is crowned king as soon as possible. This must be done if we are to further our own ambitions and add to our own fortunes."

"And what of your plans for Lady Rowena?" asked Fitzurse. "She seems to care only for her Saxon knight."

The Roar of Richard the Lion-Hearted

"I've been planning to make her my bride since I first saw her at Rotherwood. Having John in favor of this marriage only adds to my determination."

"How will you get Rowena to agree to it?"

"With an ingenious plan. I'll follow Cedric's party when they leave Ashby tonight. Then, disguised as an outlaw of the forest, I'll kidnap Rowena. Later, a brave knight will rescue her from the outlaws and carry her off to Front-de-Boeuf's castle. *I* will be that knight. It's such a romantic plan, Rowena can't possibly resist it. She'll be eager to marry me. In any event, I'll keep her at the castle until she agrees to it."

"But you can't do this alone."

"Bois-Guilbert's men will help. And now, like a true knight, I'm off to win the hand and heart of the beautiful Rowena."

As De Bracy turned to go, he didn't hear Fitzurse mutter after him, "Like a true knight? Ha! Like an utter fool!"

To Win the Hand of the Beautiful Rowena

Only the Bloody Dirt Remained.

CHAPTER 8

Kidnapped!

When Ivanhoe lost consciousness on the field, many people rushed to help him. By the time Gurth reached the spot where his master had fallen, Ivanhoe was gone, and only the bloody dirt remained.

Cedric was distressed at seeing Ivanhoe wounded, but he couldn't bring himself to go to his disinherited son in front of such a large crowd. So he sent his servant, Oswald, ordering him, "Take Ivanhoe to Ashby and find the best doctor there for him."

But Oswald didn't find Ivanhoe either;

instead, he found Gurth, who had been in such a rush to come to his master's aid, he had forgotten to hide his face with his hood. As soon as Oswald recognized him as the servant who had escaped from Rotherwood, he overpowered him and tied his hands.

"I'm taking you back to Cedric," he told Gurth as he led him off the field.

As to where Ivanhoe was, all they could learn was that the Disinherited Knight had been lifted onto a litter carried by four well-dressed servants and taken away.

Oswald caught up with Cedric's party when they stopped to rest several hours after leaving Ashby. Although Gurth pleaded to be allowed to search for Ivanhoe, Cedric said no. As long as he was certain that his son was alive and probably being cared for by friends, he planned to return home and continue his life as usual... *without his disinherited son!*

The group started up again once Oswald and Gurth had taken their places at the rear.

He Tied His Hands.

The road ahead would take them through a large forest where many bands of outlaws roamed. Cedric was certain that his ten servants, plus Oswald and Gurth, would be enough protection for Lady Rowena, her attendants, and himself.

They hadn't gone far into the forest when cries for help reached them. Riding toward the place where the cries were coming from, they saw an old man pacing back and forth, ringing his hands and moaning in terror. A young woman was on her knees reaching into a cur-tained litter on the ground.

"Thank heaven, it's you, Sir Cedric!" wept the old man. "It is I, Isaac, with my daughter Rebecca. We left Ashby with six body-guards and mules to carry our sick friend in the litter. Everything was fine until we were warned by a woodcutter of a band of outlaws up ahead. Our bodyguards ran off, taking our money and our mules. I fear we'll be attacked and mur-dered unless you protect us and let us travel

"Thank Heaven, it's You."

with you."

"We must give them servants and horses to take them to the next village," Rowena told Cedric.

But Rebecca jumped up from the litter and hurried to Rowena. "Please, my lady, I beg you to take us with you. I'm not asking for myself or for my aged father, but for the man who is near death inside this litter."

Rowena was touched by Rebecca's pleas, and she turned to Cedric. "These people need our help. We must take them with us."

Cedric couldn't deny Rowena anything, so he ordered the litter placed on two of his mules and gave Rebecca and Isaac two horses. Gurth had been left unguarded during this time, and he managed to slip away without being missed. Still, he stayed a short distance away in the forest, keeping the group in sight, hoping to learn where Ivanhoe was.

The very moment that Oswald discovered Gurth's disappearance was the moment that

Touched by Rebecca's Pleas

an attack came. Outlaws dressed in Lincoln-green tunics, with black helmets covering their faces, surrounded them.

"For merry England!" shouted the outlaws, hoping that their words and clothes would convince their victims that they were Saxon bandits who lived in this forest.

In spite of Cedric's brave defense, his party couldn't fight against so many bandits with so many weapons. In moments, they were surrounded and taken prisoner.

Gurth watched as Cedric and his party were led away. "I must go for help," he said as he turned his mule. But his way was blocked by another outlaw dressed in Lincoln-green. This outlaw, however, did not have his face hidden by a helmet.

"Who has the nerve to take prisoners here in my forest?" the outlaw demanded.

"*Your* forest? Since when does an outlaw own a forest? And who are you?" Gurth asked.

"I'm Robin of Locksley, but my men call me

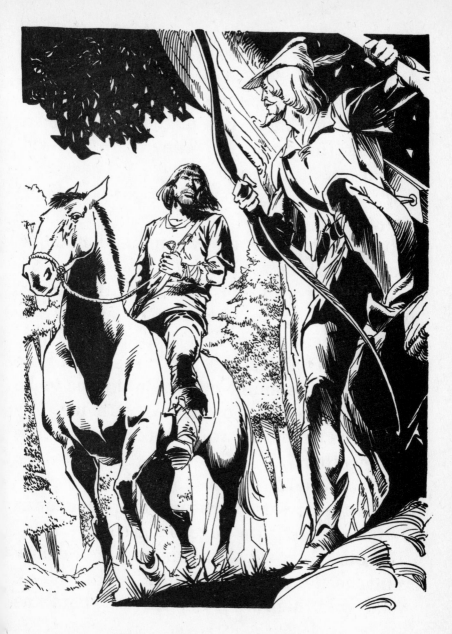

"I'm Robin of Locksley."

Robin Hood. Now tell me what happened."

"You should know, Robin. It was your men who took the prisoners. They were dressed just like you."

"*My men?* I'll see about that right now. Wait here and don't move."

Gurth waited only a few minutes for Robin to return with news.

"Good squire, I crept up behind those outlaws. They're not my men, but I learned who they are and where they're heading. They don't plan to harm any of their prisoners. But since they do outnumber us, it would be foolish to try a rescue now. Come with me. I'll gather my band and we'll make our rescue plans together."

Gurth turned his mule and followed Robin through the forest for the next three hours. When they reached a huge oak tree, five men in Lincoln-green tunics jumped up and came running to welcome their leader.

Robin told them what happened. "There's a

CHAPTER 9

Prisoners at Torquilstone

While Robin waited overnight for the arrival of his men, the mysterious outlaws were hurrying their prisoners along the road. The two leaders, still with their faces hidden, rode at the front, talking quietly.

"Isn't it time to put the second half of your plan into action, De Bracy?" asked Bois-Guilbert.

"I've changed my mind. I'm not going to put on my knight's clothes and rescue Rowena here on the road. Instead, when we get to Torquilstone, I'll confess everything to her.

She'll surely understand that my love for her drove me to take these desperate actions."

"I myself am greatly intrigued by the beautiful Rebecca," said Bois-Guilbert.

"Rebecca? I would think you'd be more interested in the beauty of her father's money bag than in the beauty of the maiden."

"I want both," sneered Bois-Guilbert. "And I'll get both. Remember, we must pay that greedy Front-de-Boeuf for using his castle."

When the party left the woods and saw the walls of Torquilstone in the distance, Cedric gasped in recognition. "We are at the very castle that King Richard gave to Ivanhoe years ago, the very same castle that Prince John gave to that brute, Front-de-Boeuf, while Ivanhoe was in the Holy Land. Now I understand. These outlaws are not English, as they pretend. They're Normans in disguise, taking us to a Norman castle!"

When the party reached the castle gate, the drawbridge was lowered to let them enter.

"They're Normans in Disguise."

Once inside the courtyard, Cedric was separated from Rowena, and Isaac was dragged from Rebecca, even though both fathers tearfully pleaded to stay with their daughters. All were separated from their servants too.

Cedric was taken to a large room, where he was treated politely by his Norman guards and served an elaborate meal.

Isaac, however, was thrown into a dungeon far below ground. As he huddled on the damp ground in one corner, he looked around him. Fastened to the walls were shackles and chains from earlier tortures and even some bones from earlier prisoners. In the middle of the floor was a large fire-pit covered with a rusty iron grate.

After several hours of sitting quietly with his hands folded in prayer, Isaac heard hinges creaking as the door was opened. The huge form of Front-de-Boeuf entered, followed by a guard carrying two large baskets.

The savage baron's cruel smile struck terror

His Hands Folded in Prayer

in the heart of the old man as he signaled the guard to open one basket. The man did so, taking out a scale and some weights, and placing them in front of Isaac.

"Isaac of York," cried Front-de-Boeuf menacingly, "on this scale you are to weigh out a thousand pounds of gold ... or face the most terrible punishment any man could imagine!"

"T-There is not that much gold in all of York or among all of my people," gasped Isaac. "Please, noble knight, have pity on me. I am old and poor and helpless."

"Old and helpless, yes. But poor? No! I warn you I will torture you long and painfully until you die. Prisoners richer and more important than you have died in this dungeon over the years and no one ever knew what became of them."

Front-de-Boeuf then gave orders to his guard. "Empty the coals from the other basket into the fire-pit and strike the flint and steel together to get the sparks to light them. Then

"I Will Torture You Long and Painfully!"

fan the fire with the bellows until the coals are red-hot."

Once the coals were glowing and the guard had replaced the grate on top of the pit, Front-de-Boeuf turned back to Isaac. "See that grate, old man? It's becoming red-hot, a red-hot bed for you to lie on until you slowly burn to death. That is your choice—a fiery death or the gold I demand!"

"I don't have that much gold!"

With a cruel smile, the baron ordered, "Seize him and toss him on the grate!"

"No, wait! I'll pay," screamed Isaac. "But I'll have to go to my countrymen and beg and borrow that huge amount."

"I won't allow you to leave here. The gold must be delivered to this dungeon before you can be set free."

"And when it's delivered, will my daughter and our sick friend and everyone in Cedric's party be freed too?"

"Their ransom isn't up to me. It's being

"Toss Him on the Grate!"

decided upon by others in the castle."

"If you won't let me leave, you must permit my daughter Rebecca to go to York to borrow the gold for me."

"Rebecca is your daughter? . . . But I can't let her go. She is Brian de Bois-Guilbert's prisoner. She belongs to him just as if he won her from a challenger in a tournament."

"No! No! No!" shrieked Isaac as if his whole body were being burnt over the fire at that very moment. "Torture me, burn me, but spare my daughter. The Templar is evil. He's a cruel knight who will dishonor her!"

"Dog! How dare you insult as fine a knight as Bois-Guilbert!"

"Do what you will with me, robber and villain! I will pay you nothing unless Rebecca is returned to me safely. She is a thousand times dearer to me than my own body!"

"Then your cursed old body shall be thrown on the bed of fire, Isaac of York!"

"A Thousand Times Dearer to Me!"

"A Prisoner of Your Beauty"

CHAPTER 10

Surprise Visitors

The Lady Rowena had been taken to the only chamber decent enough for a Saxon princess.

She remained alone there for several hours until Maurice De Bracy entered, now dressed in knightly finery. He bowed, then reached out his arm to lead Rowena to a seat.

"I prefer to stand in the company of my jailer, Sir Knight," snapped Rowena.

"I'm not your jailer, fair lady, but a prisoner of your beauty."

"I do not know you, sir, and you have no

right to speak to a lady in such a familiar way, especially one you have kidnapped while you were disguised. Your courteous tongue does not forgive your evil deed. I want nothing to do with a man such as you."

De Bracy was confused that Rowena was offended by his gallant compliment, so he resumed his arrogant Norman ways. "Since you don't welcome my polite language, I shall be forced to speak more boldly. You shall *never* leave this castle, Lady Rowena, unless it is as the bride of Maurice de Bracy!"

"Never!"

"Don't be so quick to reject me, my lady. And don't hold out hopes that you'll be the bride of your beloved Ivanhoe, for at this very minute he's a prisoner in this castle too."

"Ivanhoe here? You're lying!"

"No, my lady. I recognized him as he was carried in on his litter. But only *I* know his true identity. One word to Front-de-Boeuf, however, and Ivanhoe is a dead man. The

"I Want Nothing To Do with You."

baron will stop at nothing, even murder, to keep this castle as his own. Now shall I go to Front-de-Boeuf to prove it to you?"

"No, no, please don't do that! I believe you. Save Ivanhoe, I beg you!"

"Only by agreeing to marry me can you save his life and free yourself from this castle. If you refuse, you'll remain a prisoner and both Ivanhoe *and* Cedric will die."

At the added threat against her beloved guardian's life, Rowena's courage left her, and she burst into hysterical weeping.

De Bracy began to pace back and forth helplessly. ""I can't bear the pain I've caused this beautiful woman," he said to himself. "How I wish I was as hard-hearted as Front-de-Boeuf! What am I do without losing face among my friends?"

Meanwhile, Rebecca had been taken to a small room high in a turret. Her first act had been to inspect the room, searching for a way to escape, but the window led only to a

High in a Turret

parapet, or balcony, outside the turret.

Rebecca was a strong-willed, courageous young woman, but she began to tremble when the door opened and one of the kidnappers entered. His cap was pulled down over the upper half of his face, and he held his cloak over the lower half.

When the outlaw just stood there, without saying a word, Rebecca guessed at what he wanted. She hurriedly took two bracelets off her arm and unclasped her necklace. "Take these," she said, reaching them out to the man, "and be merciful to my father and me."

"Beautiful lady, these diamonds cannot sparkle as magnificently as your eyes do. It is not diamonds or gold that I seek, for your father will provide all the gold we need. No, you must pay your ransom with your beauty and your love."

"You're no outlaw!" cried Rebecca, "No outlaw would refuse such jewels. You're a Norman. Uncover yourself if you dare!"

"You're No Outlaw!"

"You have guessed," said Brian de Bois-Guilbert, dropping his cloak from his face. "And truly, I have no need for your jewels. Rather, I would be pleased to add many more to your beautiful neck and arms."

"What can you want of me? We have nothing in common. You are a Christian and I am a Jewess. We could never marry."

Bois-Guilbert laughed mockingly. "Marry a Jewess? Never! Besides, my vows as a Templar prevent me from marrying anyone. But those vows do not prevent me from loving you as a man loves a woman."

"How dare you offend me! May God forgive you for suggesting such a vile thing!"

"I don't need you to scold me," snapped Bois-Guilbert, his eyes flashing. "You forget that you are my prisoner and I have the right to take from you anything I wish."

"Stand back, Sir Knight!" cried Rebecca. "If you overpower me, I will renounce you all over Europe. I will shame you among your Christ-

"Stand Back, Sir Knight!"

ian friends for having sinned with a Jewess."

"What you say is true, but who will hear your voice outside the walls of this castle? No, Rebecca, only three things can save you. Give up your religion, become a Christian, and accept my love."

"I spit at you, vile knight! Give up my religion? Never! My God has given me a way to escape from you." And Rebecca threw open the window and ran to the edge of the parapet, where she stood ready to jump off.

Taken by surprise, Bois-Guilbert followed after to stop her. "Wait!" he shouted.

"Stop where you are, cruel knight. If you come one step closer, I'll throw myself off this parapet. I'd rather be crushed in the courtyard below than be the victim of your brutality." As she said this, Rebecca threw her hands up towards heaven as if asking for God's mercy before she jumped.

Bois-Guilbert admired Rebecca's strength and courage. "Come down, reckless girl," he

Ready to Jump Off

said gently. "I promise I will not offend you ever again."

"I don't trust you."

"I swear I will not harm you. If you won't come off that ledge for *your* sake, then do it for your father's. Please don't be afraid of me. Let me be your friend. And perhaps one day, when you know me better, you might learn to love me."

Rebecca sensed an honesty in the Templar's words. "I'll trust you for now," she said as she got down off the ledge.

Just then, a bugle call sounded outside the castle. "I must go now and see what news that messenger brings." And Bois-Guilbert hurried from the parapet.

Shaken at having come so close to death, Rebecca stumbled back inside and dropped to her knees in prayer. "Thank You, God, for protecting me. And please give Your protection to my father and Ivanhoe as well."

Dropped to Her Knees in Prayer

A Challenge from the Black Knight

CHAPTER 11

Switched Identities

The bugle call that brought Bois-Guilbert in from the parapet also gave De Bracy an excuse to leave his embarrassing situation in Rowena's room. It also interrupted Front-de-Boeuf's cruel plans for torturing Isaac.

The three Normans met in the great hall, where a guard brought in the letter delivered by the messenger.

Bois-Guilbert grabbed the letter and read aloud, *"I, the Black Knight who challenged you at Ashby, demand that you release the prisoners you kidnapped. If you do not release them within one hour, Robin of Locksley and I have hundreds of men ready to attack Torquilstone and destroy you."*

The three men stared at each other in disbelief. Front-de-Boeuf was the first to speak. "These outlaws not only outnumber us, but they hate me as well. I've been punishing them all these years when I catch them in my forest where they hunt for food."

"Then let's not wait till they come at us," suggested De Bracy. "Let's attack them first."

"We don't have enough men to do that and also guard the castle," said Front-de-Boeuf. "Can't we get any help from your friends in nearby castles?" asked Bois-Guilbert.

"They're all in York for John's coronation where we should be too. But perhaps we can send a messenger to the prince or to them."

"And have him captured by those outlaws when he enters the forest?" argued De Bracy.

"I have a plan that will get our message through safely," said Front-de-Boeuf. Then he

"They Hate Me."

quickly wrote a return message: *The prisoners are ours and we will not release them. We plan to execute Cedric at dawn, so send in a priest to hear his final confession.*

"Take this letter to the messenger outside," Front-de-Boeuf told his guard.

Within the hour, that letter was delivered to Robin, Gurth, and the Black Knight at the big oak tree. By now, hundreds of Robin's men had gathered, along with many neighboring towns-people and all the servants from Rotherwood.

The Black Knight read the message, then offered his plan. "I don't think they'll execute Cedric immediately. But since they want a priest, we can have one of our men enter the castle in that disguise. He can bring word back to us as to their defenses."

Gurth had an even better plan. "Let *me* go in as a priest. I'll look over their defenses and also try to rescue Cedric. I owe it to him and to my young master Ivanhoe, wherever he might be."

"Let *Me* Go in as a Priest"

Robin agreed to let Gurth try. He called to Tuck, "Give Gurth your robe, good friar."

Tuck removed his robe and pulled it over Gurth's head. As he tied a rope belt around the squire's waist and hung a heavy cross around his neck, he gave him a few words of advice. "No matter what any of those Normans ask you, just answer with two words in a deep, serious voice, *'Pax vobiscum.'* That's Latin for 'Peace be with you.'"

"Pax vobiscum," practiced Gurth as he got on his mule and set off for Torquilstone.

Gurth next repeated his *Pax vobiscum* to cover his trembling knees as he stood before Front-de-Boeuf, explaining, "I'm a poor monk who was attacked by a band of thieves in the forest. They forced me to come here to hear a dying man's final confession."

"And how many thieves were in this band, holy father?" asked Front-de-Boeuf.

"Hundreds, even thousands! *I* even feared for my life," lied the pretended friar.

"I'm a Poor Monk."

"What!" cried Bois-Guilbert, entering the room. "We must send for help immediately. I'll write the message and have this holy man deliver it when he leaves here."

A servant led the friar to Cedric's room. At a nod from the friar, he left them alone.

"Pax vobiscum," said Gurth in a deep, serious voice as he pulled his hood over his face. "I have come to prepare you for death, noble Cedric."

"What! Wicked as these Normans are, they wouldn't dare put me to death!"

"I fear they have no conscience, my son."

"Then I shall die like a man," declared Cedric, and he knelt down to pray.

"Look and listen first, noble master," said Gurth, resuming his normal voice and pushing back the hood of his robe.

"Gurth!" gasped Cedric. "What are you doing here, and in the robe of a holy man?"

"Don't ask me anything. Just put on my robe and leave this castle immediately. I'll put on

"Gurth! What Are You Doing Here?"

your cloak and cap, and stay here in your place."

"I can't leave you here. They'd hang you! And I can't leave without Rowena and the rest of my party. Isn't there a chance of rescue for all of us?"

"Yes. Five hundred men are waiting to attack this castle, but they need your help."

"But how can I get out?" argued Cedric. "How will I answer a Norman who might stop me? I don't know any priestly language."

"Two words will get you past any Norman. *Pax vobiscum.* Just say it in a deep, serious voice. And if someone tries any more Latin on you, just pretend you're deaf."

Cedric finally nodded tearfully and let Gurth put the robe on him. He hugged the brave young man, then rushed from the room. When he reached the hallway, Cedric found Front-de-Boeuf waiting, a paper in his hand.

"Sir Friar, those thieves outside the castle must be prevented from attacking us. Carry

Cedric Nodded Tearfully.

this letter to the prince at York."

The friar nodded, then mumbled his *Pax vobiscum* and hurried to join Robin and the Black Knight in the woods. On the way, he tore up the letter and threw it in the moat.

Inside the castle, Front-de-Boeuf ordered Cedric brought before him. The man who was led in had his cap pulled down over his face and stood in a shadowy part of the room to avoid being recognized.

"Well, gallant Saxon, how are you enjoying our hospitality at Torquilstone?" sneered Front-de-Boeuf. "Are you interested in paying a ransom to save your worthless life or shall I hang you upside down from the iron bars of the castle window?"

"I don't have one cent for ransom, Baron. And since my memory hasn't been too good lately, perhaps hanging me upside down will improve my brain."

"What kind of nonsense is that?" cried Front-de-Boeuf, pushing the cap off Gurth's

"What Kind of Nonsense is That?"

head. "Who are you?"

"I can answer that," said De Bracy, entering the room. "He's Cedric's servant, the one who ran off to become Ivanhoe's squire."

The baron then turned to his guard. "You fool! Go and bring me the real Cedric!"

"'But, Sir, no one else was in the room."

"Good Lord!" cried De Bracy. "Cedric must have escaped in the friar's robe!"

"And you," screamed Front-de-Boeuf, lunging at Gurth, "I'll tear your head from your body and throw you off the castle walls!"

"Calm yourself," said De Bracy. "He's only a simple peasant and not worth killing."

"You seem to forget, De Bracy, that because of him, our message will never reach York. We'll never get help from anyone."

"Then it's time for us to prepare for an attack and not stand here talking. Summon Bois-Guilbert and let's position our men."

From their place on the wall, the three Norman knights looked out over the forest

"Go and Bring Me the Real Cedric."

surrounding the castle.

Bois-Guilbert pointed into the distance and said, "Those men are very well organized. They've taken cover behind every tree and bush, and never once have they exposed themselves within the shooting range of our bows. I'm certain they're being led by some noble knight or gentleman highly skilled in the art of war."

"I think I see such a leader," said De Bracy. "Look, in the distance, at the tall man in black armor. It's the Black Knight who came to Ivanhoe's aid at Ashby and who defeated Front-de-Boeuf and me."

"And since he disappeared right after his victory before I could challenge him again, I shall have my revenge on him now!" swore the baron.

So, as the Saxons approached Torquilstone, the Normans got ready for their attack.

"It's the Black Knight."

"Brave Knight!"

CHAPTER 12

The Attack on Torquilstone

When the prisoners first arrived at Torquil-stone, the litter carrying Isaac's "sick friend" was taken to a turret room just beyond Rebecca's. Once Bois-Guilbert had left her room, the young woman hurried to the wounded knight and bent over the unconscious form of Ivanhoe.

"How pale and weak you are from losing so much blood, brave knight!" she whispered as she began changing his bloody bandages.

Ivanhoe's eyes fluttered for a moment, then focused on the beautiful young woman.

"W-Where am I?" he muttered in confusion. "And w-who are you?"

"I am Rebecca, daughter of Isaac of York, the man you saved from cruel robbers. My father's servants carried you off the field at Ashby after you fainted, and we brought you to the inn where we were staying. It was there that I began treating your wounds."

"You? A woman?" Ivanhoe was amazed.

"Don't doubt my ability, Sir Knight. I learned the art of healing from Miriam, the most respected woman in our tribe. I've spent my life using that knowledge to heal my people as well as yours."

"Then I thank you, my dear Rebecca. But tell me, are we still at the inn at Ashby?"

"No, while you were unconscious, but with your bleeding slowed down, we decided to set out for our home in York, where I had all my medicines and salves with which to properly treat you. We made you comfortable in my litter, and you were making the journey very well

"I am Rebecca."

until the men we hired to carry the litter took our mules and ran off."

"Then w-what—? H-How—? W-Where?"

"Cedric's party found us and permitted us to travel with them. But not long after, we were attacked by a band of outlaws, who turned out to be hateful Norman knights in disguise. They brought us here to Torquilstone, then separated us—Cedric, his servants, your squire Gurth, my father, and—"

"Good Lord! Rowena too?" cried Ivanhoe, pushing himself up and groaning in pain.

Rebecca nodded. "Yes, the Lady Rowena too. She is in another part of the castle."

"Then I must—I must—" But the effort to rise was too much for Ivanhoe, and he fell back, exhausted, and was soon asleep again.

"Rest well, brave knight." And Rebecca bent down to kiss Ivanhoe's pale cheek.

Rebecca never moved from Ivanhoe's side during the hours that the Black Knight and his men were preparing for the attack, the same

"Rest Well!"

hours that the Norman commanders spent on the walls watching those preparations.

When Ivanhoe finally stirred again, his strength seemed to be returning. "Thank you, dear Rebecca, my gentle doctor," he said. "Has our situation changed at all?"

"Our Norman captors have spent many hours making preparations to defend the castle. When I stepped out on the parapet and looked towards the woods, I saw hundreds of armed Saxons. They seemed to be taking their orders from the same Black Knight who came to your aid at Ashby."

"If only I could be there with them," Ivanhoe muttered impatiently. "The bugle signals the beginning of the attack. Listen! Hear the shouts, the whiz of arrows flying through the air, the crashing of rocks being hurled down from the battlements. I must—"

"You mustn't even *think* of getting up, Ivanhoe. You've lost too much blood; you're too weak. I'll stand at the window and tell you

"Hear the Shouts, the Whiz of Arrows."

everything that's happening."

"No! You mustn't!" cried Ivanhoe. "An arrow could hit you at any moment. Please, Rebecca, you mustn't risk injury or death."

But Rebecca knew how important the battle was to Ivanhoe, so she ignored his warnings and ran up the two steps leading to the latticed window. "They're advancing now. I see hundreds of them, the first line with huge shields and wooden battering rams, and behind them, archers loading their long-bows, shooting, and reloading. Arrows are flying in such a heavy attack that I can barely see the bowmen who shot them."

"The attack can't go on this way," said Ivanhoe in frustration. "Saxon arrows won't pierce and collapse stone walls. The castle must be stormed by pure force."

"Wait! I think the Black Knight is doing just that. His men are smashing the gate with their battle-axes and a battering ram.... The barricade's down! They're rushing in.... Oh,

Smashing the Gate with Battle Axes

no! The Normans are running out, pushing them back.... Now the Black Knight and Front-de-Boeuf are facing each other, swinging, lunging, slashing. Front-de-Boeuf is down. He's not moving.... Bois-Guilbert is dragging his body inside the walls."

"And our forces?"

"They have ladders up against the outer walls, but the Normans are hurling rocks and tree trunks down on them. Still the Black Knight fights, harder than any man there. Rocks and tree trunks can't stop him!"

"There is only one man in all of England who can fight like that!" cried Ivanhoe, as he joyfully raised his weak body to a sitting position. "Only one man whose heart and arm fight with that kind of strength for the love of England and his people!"

"Wait! They're dropping a long raft across the moat to make a floating bridge.... Now they're crossing it.... They're inside the gates and up on the battlements.... Wait! The

"Only One Man in All of England."

Normans are fleeing back into the castle."

When the two Norman leaders met inside the hall, De Bracy reported, "On my side of the wall, Robin Hood led his archers in a heavy attack, but we held our position."

Bois-Guilbert shook his head. "I couldn't hold mine. The baron is dead. Do you think we can still defend Torquilstone?"

"Hardly. We're greatly outnumbered, and I fear we'll have to give up our prisoners if we hope to escape with our lives."

"Shame on you, De Bracy! We'd be ridiculed till our dying day. I'd rather die here than be dishonored. To the walls! Let us fight!"

But as they ran from the hall, their way was blocked by a wall of smoke and flames.

"The fire is coming up from the dungeon!" cried Bois-Guilbert. "The entire western side of the castle is in flames."

"The stupidity of Front-de-Boeuf! The fire must have spread from the dungeon pit where he was planning to torture Isaac."

"The Castle is in Flames."

And so it had, with a little help from the shrewd old man. For when his guards heard the Saxons attacking the western side of the castle, they ran off. Left alone, Isaac saw his chance to divert the Normans' attention from fighting Saxons to fighting fires. So he began tossing into the pit anything he could find that would burn—chairs, tables, planks, rags, straw—before he made his own escape from the dungeon.

When De Bracy realized that the fire was out of control and blocking most of the exits, he shouted, "What are we to do?"

"We must get our men out the rear gate," cried Bois-Guilbert. "It's the only entrance where there's been no fighting. Hurry!"

Minutes later, De Bracy and Bois-Guilbert flung open the gate, only to crash into the Black Knight. The Norman soldiers behind them drew back in fear.

De Bracy screamed at them, "Dogs! Are you such cowards that you let one man frighten

Tossing Things into the Pit

IVANHOE

you and block your only escape?"

"That man is the devil!" cried one guard.

"Get out of my way then!" raged De Bracy. "I'll face him myself."

Maurice De Bracy and the Black Knight fought hand to hand, each dealing furious blows with his sword on the other. Finally, one blow from the Black Knight landed with such force that De Bracy fell to the ground.

Bending over him, his dagger against the Norman's throat, the Black Knight demanded, "Give up, De Bracy, or you're a dead man!"

"Give up to an unknown victor? Ha! I won't be dishonored by admitting I was defeated by a nameless peasant! So, either tell me who you are or go ahead and kill me!"

The Black Knight knelt closer to De Bracy whispered something in his ear.

Maurice De Bracy's defiance disappeared and he meekly admitted, "I give up."

"Then turn yourself over to my men at the drawbridge. I'll deal with you later."

"I Give Up."

"Before I go, I think you'd like to know that Ivanhoe is a prisoner here. He's badly wounded and as soon as the fire spreads, he'll be trapped in the burning castle."

"Ivanhoe a prisoner? In danger of dying? Quickly, tell me where he is."

The instant De Bracy pointed to a winding stairway, the Black Knight was gone. De Bracy then headed to the drawbridge, where many of his men were surrendering to Cedric and Robin Hood.

Meanwhile, the fire was spreading and smoke was beginning to seep into Ivanhoe's room. Rebecca was still at the window when she heard shouts of "Water! Water!"

She ran to the door, but faced a wall of flames. "The castle's on fire!" she cried.

"You must save yourself, Rebecca," begged Ivanhoe. "You can't worry about me."

"I refuse to leave you. If we're both not rescued, I'll die with you. . . . And yet, oh God, my father! What will happen to him?"

"You Must Save Yourself."

At that moment, the door was flung open and Bois-Guilbert crashed into the room. His broken and bloody armor was charred from the flames. "I'm here to save you, Rebecca. Follow me quickly. I'll lead you to safety."

"I'll go only if you save my father and this wounded knight as well."

"A knight must be prepared to meet death no matter how, and I don't much care how an old man dies either. Now come!"

"Beast! I would rather die in this fire than be rescued by a savage like you!"

"You have no choice, Rebecca." And Bois-Guilbert picked up the terrified young woman, who shrieked and clawed at his face as he carried her out of the room.

"Dog!" cried Ivanhoe. "Put her down! I'll kill you for this."

Moments later, the Black Knight burst into the room. "Thank God you're safe, Ivanhoe." And he picked up the young knight as easily as Bois-Guilbert had lifted Rebecca and

"You Have No Choice, Rebecca."

carried him to the rear gate and to safety.

Leaving Ivanhoe in the care of two of his men, the Black Knight went back into the castle to rescue the other prisoners.

Saxons ran from room to room, searching out the Norman defenders. Many had already fled. Those who resisted felt the blade of Saxon swords, and only those who surrendered left the castle alive.

Amid all this confusion, Cedric rushed about in search of Rowena. He found her in her room, kneeling in prayer, preparing to meet her death. He hurried her out of the smoke-filled room and down to safety.

The Norman who had been ordered to guard Gurth discovered the smoke as it crept into the room. Afraid of being trapped, the man rushed for the nearest stairway, leaving the room unlocked. Gurth then had no trouble escaping down into the courtyard.

In the middle of the courtyard, Brian de Bois-Guilbert was mounting his horse and

Preparing To Meet Her Death

placing Rebecca in front of him. He was surrounded by several of his men who were protecting their leader as he made his escape.

Saxons were coming at him from all sides, their bows ready to shoot. Bois-Guilbert spurred his horse into a gallop across the drawbridge, calling back, "Your bows are useless, Saxon archers! You dare not shoot for fear of hitting Rebecca!"

At that moment, Friar Tuck and several of Robin's band stepped out into the courtyard. "We went down to the cellar to rescue some good food and wine from the fire, and look who we found wandering through the hallway, looking for the way out." And he gripped the arm of Isaac of York, who was gasping for air as he stumbled across the stone floor.

The old man lifted his eyes in time to see two riders crossing the drawbridge on one horse. He clutched at his breast as tears filled his eyes and rolled down his cheeks. "My child! My Rebecca!"

"My Child! My Rebecca!"

A Pile of Burnt Wood and Stone.

CHAPTER 13

De Bracy Brings News to Prince John

From the edge of the forest, the victorious Saxons and their Norman prisoners gazed in wonder as the towering flames lit up the evening sky. Before the fire burned itself out, Torquilstone Castle had collapsed to the ground, a pile of burnt wood and stone.

After several minutes, Robin spoke to the Black Knight and Cedric. "My men gathered many treasures from the castle before the fire got out of control. I want to divide them evenly and reward our men as well."

"I have no need of any further treasures," replied Cedric, "and I am able to reward my men from my own wealth."

"And I," added the Black Knight, "ask only that Maurice de Bracy be given to me as my prisoner, to do with as I wish."

Robin nodded. "I'll do as you ask, but I'd prefer to hang the Norman dog!"

"Thank you, Robin," said the Black Knight as he wheeled his horse around and made his way towards De Bracy.

"You are free," he told the Norman. "I'll take no revenge against you if you leave England at once. But if you ever return to this land, you will pay for your crimes with your life."

De Bracy bowed to the Black Knight, then leaped onto the back of a horse rescued from Front-de-Boeuf's stables and set off for York. He was loyal enough to Prince John to want to warn him not to proceed with the ceremonies crowning himself king.

De Bracy rode all night and reached York

"You Are Free."

the following morning. By then, reports had reached Prince John that his three trusted Norman knights had been killed or taken prisoner at Torquilstone as the result of De Bracy's foolish kidnapping scheme.

"If those three knights are still alive, I'll hang them!" John raged to Fitzurse. "They were to be here to support me at my coronation, not disrupt it by some ridiculous kidnapping to impress a Saxon woman!"

"Just remember, Your Highness, that if they *are* alive, they'll be important friends and could be dangerous enemies."

"Yes, yes, yes," replied John impatiently. "But we'll find out soon enough. There's De Bracy entering the hall now."

"Good God!" cried Fitzurse. "He's covered with blood and dirt. The battle must have been terrible. Try to hide your anger."

Prince John stood to welcome De Bracy. "What news do you bring, my loyal knight?"

"Bad news, I fear. Front-de-Boeuf is dead

"He's Covered with Blood and Dirt."

and Bois-Guilbert has fled with Rebecca of York. But I have worse news, Your Highness. Your brother Richard is in England, alive."

Prince John's knees buckled under him, and he clutched a chair for support. "You're mad, De Bracy! What you say is impossible!"

"No, Your Highness. I spoke with him myself. He's been disguised so no one knew who he was. But he revealed his identity to me."

"Where is he now?"

"With the outlaw band that attacked and destroyed Torquilstone."

"Then you must capture him before he returns to claim the throne!"

"I? No, Your Highness. I've been warned to leave England under penalty of death, and I'll flee to France now that I've done my duty to you. I'd advise you to escape as well, rather than suffer the shame or even death that Richard would inflict on you."

"Leave at once, coward! I have no need for knights who refuse to do my bidding!"

"You're Mad, De Bracy!"

Once De Bracy had bowed and gone, Prince John turned to Fitzurse. "And now, my good Waldemar, will you, too, fail me or do you have the loyalty and courage to find Richard the Lion-Hearted and see to it that he never reaches York alive?"

Waldemar Fitzurse saw an opportunity to further ensure his rise to power as Chancellor once John was crowned king. So he bowed low and replied, "While I am not a violent man, Your Highness, my loyalty to you and my promise to help you gain the throne require me to do what you ask. I will summon my most trusted men and carry out your orders."

Even though Fitzurse had been his trusted advisor, by now Prince John was so crazed, he was doubting everyone's loyalty. As the man turned his back and left the hall, John muttered to himself, "If you betray me, Waldemar Fitzurse, I'll have your head, even if Richard were breaking down the doors of my castle while I was doing it!"

He Was Doubting Everyone's Loyalty.

"It's Bois-Gilbert and Rebecca."

CHAPTER 14

Accused of Sorcery!

Prince John spent the entire day pacing nervously in his private apartment and the entire night tossing and turning in his bed. The following morning, Fitzurse entered the hall with more surprising news. "Your Highness, you have more visitors today."

"I don't care to see anyone!"

"I think you'll want to see these two. It's Bois-Guilbert and Rebecca."

"Bring them both in. Now maybe we'll find out what really happened at Torquilstone."

Prince John hid his anger as he welcomed

the Templar. "Sir Brian, how glad I am to see that you escaped unharmed from the fires at Torquilstone. But why did you take the daughter of Isaac with you?"

"I love this woman and didn't want any harm to come to her."

"Harm!" cried Rebecca angrily. "You kidnapped me and are holding me prisoner."

At that moment, Fitzurse whispered something to the prince, and John turned to Rebecca. "I am told that you are a sorceress, a witch with great powers. Why couldn't you use those powers to escape from this knight?"

"I am *not* a sorceress, Your Highness. I use my healing powers only to ease the pain of the sick and wounded. My medicines and ointments are made with ingredients that respected Jewish physicians have been using for centuries to cure your people and mine. I was taught to use them by Miriam, who—"

"—Who was accused of witchcraft and burned at the stake!" shouted Fitzurse.

"I Am *Not* a Sorceress."

"She was *not* a witch! Nor am I."

"But surely you must be," said John, smiling cruelly. "Look at how you have enchanted one of the bravest and most loyal knights in all of England. Why, he risked his life rescuing you from the fire and now he risks his reputation by bringing you here."

"That is true, Your Highness," admitted Bois-Guilbert. "I *did* risk my life and my honor. I confessed my love to Rebecca and she rejected me. Even now she continues to reject me. What am I to do?"

"The matter is not for you to decide, Sir Brian," Prince John said firmly. "I decree that this woman is to be brought to trial tomorrow morning on charges of witchcraft."

Even Fitzurse was shocked at the speed with which the prince was scheduling the trial. Then he thought to himself, "I guess a trial can proceed rapidly when the judge has already decided on the verdict and the sentence in advance." But he leaned over to the

Charges of Witchcraft.

prince and whispered, "Do we have enough evidence against this woman to convict her?"

"Find witnesses who will testify to her sorcery, even if you have to pay them to lie about it," John whispered back. Then aloud, he ordered, "Guards, lock this woman in a room and see to it that no one, not even Sir Brian de Bois-Guilbert, talks to her."

"But Your Highness," protested the Templar, "I love this woman. If it please—"

"Say no more, Sir Brian. I am doing what is best for your honor and for England. Be here for the sorceress's trial tomorrow. . . . And you, Fitzurse, see to it that all of York is notified of this trial, all the nobles and peasants. I'll show them just how brilliant and powerful a king I can be!"

"Actually stupid and weak," thought Fitzurse. "But with a brilliant and powerful chancellor like me at his side, no one need ever know!"

"Actually Stupid and Weak."

Crowding To See the Witch

CHAPTER 15

Demand a Trial by Combat

The castle bell tolled eight when the guards unlocked Rebecca's door and led the young woman to the great hall. Seated on a raised throne was Prince John, with Fitzurse at his side. Below him were seats for the Norman knights already in York for his coronation. Those seats were all filled, except the one reserved for Brian de Bois-Guilbert.

Along both sides of the long hall were wooden benches for the peasants. But as Rebecca was being led in, they were on their feet, crowding to see the witch. As she passed through them, her head down and her arms at her sides, Rebecca felt a piece of paper being pushed into her hand. She didn't look to see who had passed it to her or what was written on it. She was just grateful at the thought that somewhere in this crowd, she had a friend.

At the same moment that Rebecca was seated on a small wooden bench in the center of the hall, Bois-Guilbert slid into his seat in the row of knights.

At a signal from Prince John, Waldemar Fitzurse unrolled a scroll and began to read. "By order of John, Prince of England, we have summoned before us Rebecca of York on charges of witchcraft and sorcery, and of using those powers to put under her spell a true and honest knight of the finest order, Sir Brian de Bois-Guilbert."

The first witness, a castle guard, told such an exaggerated story of Bois-Guilbert's bravery during the fire that he swore, "The knight must have been under the spell of some

Unrolling a Scroll

supernatural power, like a witch's."

The next witness, a poor peasant, was dragged in on crutches. He tearfully testified that years ago an illness had left him bedridden, but after Rebecca treated him, he was able to walk again, even though it was on crutches. "She meant me no harm. She treated me no differently because I am a Christian than she treated her own people, and she even gave me a supply of that ointment to use on my weak legs." And the man reached into his tunic and took out a tin.

Fitzurse grabbed the tin and passed it to two of the king's medical advisors—one, a monk and the other, a barber. The men examined the ointment, which was nothing more than a mixture of some herbs, but they were unable to identify it. Not wanting to admit their ignorance, they reported to Fitzurse, "It is no ointment known to man. It must have been given to that woman by the devil!"

Gasps of horror passed among the crowd.

Ointments from the Devil!

Heads nodded and fingers pointed at the accused woman.

The next witness was a soldier who testified, "I saw her bending over a wounded man at Torquilstone. She made some magical signs over his wounds and chanted some mysterious words. Suddenly, the iron tip of an arrow popped out of his wound without a drop of blood showing. Moments later, the wound was healed as if it had never been there. The dying man then stood up and stepped out onto the parapet to help us defend the castle."

"And were there any other incidents of this woman's sorcery?" asked Fitzurse.

"Yes, I saw another. The witch was standing on the edge of the parapet outside her window. I thought she was going to jump, even though Sir Brian de Bois-Guilbert was with her. Then suddenly, she changed herself into a black swan and flew around the castle three times. When she landed once more on the parapet, she changed back into a woman."

Fingers Pointed at the Accused Woman!

This time, the crowd was stunned into silence, afraid that if they whispered even one word, the witch would enchant them.

Fitzurse broke the silence. "You have heard the evidence against you, Rebecca of York. Before Prince John pronounces your sentence, do you have anything to say?"

Rebecca stood proudly and spoke with dignity. "I have committed no crime by relieving the suffering of the sick or wounded, whether they be Christians or Jews. And certainly you, Sir Brian, know that these monstrous accusations are lies. On your honor as a knight, will you not speak up for me?"

Bois-Guilbert's face twisted in pain as he looked from Rebecca to Prince John. What was more important—his love for this fearless young woman or his loyalty to Prince John and his honor among his fellow knights? He knew he couldn't change the verdict, but there was a chance of changing Rebecca's death sentence—the cruel, slow torture of being burned

"Will You Not Speak Up for Me?"

at the stake!

In a voice barely above a whisper, Bois-Guilbert said, "The paper! The paper!"

"Aha!" cried Fitzurse. "That's more proof. The knight is so bewitched by this woman, he can only babble about some paper. She must have a magic spell written on some paper."

But Rebecca understood what Bois-Guilbert meant. She looked down at the piece of paper hidden in her hand and silently read the words on it: *Demand a trial by combat*. She quickly crumpled it without being seen and tucked it into the sleeve of her dress. Then lifting her head high, she spoke in a proud, clear voice. "I still swear that I am innocent, that the accusations against me are all lies. I have only one chance left to save my life according to your laws of chivalry, and that chance is by demanding a trial by combat. If someone will come forth and fight on my behalf and win, I shall be set free. If not, I am prepared to die."

As she said that, Rebecca tore off her glove

"The Paper! The Paper!"

and threw it at Prince John's feet—a challenge that couldn't be refused.

Prince John picked up the glove with an evil laugh. "I accept this challenge. The prisoner has three days in which to find someone to defend her against my own Champion. To defend the honor of the crown, I now name the noble knight, Sir Brian de Bois-Guilbert!"

The Templar shuddered and thought, "How cruel of him to choose me! How can I live with myself, knowing I'll be the one who'll send the woman I love to her death?"

The crippled peasant, who had been forced to testify, offered to carry Rebecca's plea to Isaac. "Tell my father that the one man who would surely face Bois-Guilbert as my Champion is Ivanhoe. But I fear he is still too weak to fight. So, if my father can't find anyone else, I shall die with courage."

A Challenge that Couldn't Be Refused.

"I know I Must Leave."

CHAPTER 16

The Final Battle

After the Black Knight rescued Ivanhoe from the burning castle, Gurth took him to a convent to rest while his wounds healed. Rebecca's ointments had been so effective that after only a few days, Ivanhoe was on his feet and anxious to leave. He explained to Gurth, "I have a strange feeling that something evil is about to happen. I can't explain it, but I know I must leave."

Gurth had almost convinced Ivanhoe to rest for one more day when a messenger rode in with an urgent letter from Isaac for him.

"My premonition of evil has come to pass," said Ivanhoe after reading the letter. "I must leave immediately and ride hard if I am to reach York in time to to help Rebecca."

So Ivanhoe set off for York, where a field of combat and death was already set up outside the castle walls. Galleries and benches had been built for the spectators. Piles of dried sticks had been heaped around a stake where a witch would be burned.

At dawn, church bells summoned everyone. Peasants and lesser nobles crowded into their seats. A trumpet announced the entry of the royal procession. Prince John rode in first, followed by Bois-Guilbert and high-ranking nobles and knights.

Behind the riders walked the prisoner, in a plain white dress. All of her jewelry had been taken from her for fear that some of it contained charms with which she could summon powers from the devil. She held her head high and her face showed dignity and courage.

A Royal Procession

She was led to a black chair placed in front of the funeral pyre. Before she sat down, she glanced at the stake, then shut her eyes and shuddered.

After a flourish of the trumpets, a herald stepped forward and announced, "Hear ye! Hear ye! Here stands Sir Brian de Bois-Guilbert ready to do battle with any challenger who comes forth to defend Rebecca of York."

The trumpets sounded again. Then silence. And more silence. No challenger appeared.

"We've waited three days for a challenger. We'll wait one more hour," said Prince John, "to show that I *am* a fair and just ruler."

During that hour, Rebecca's eyes were fixed on the ground. She didn't raise them until Bois-Guilbert rode towards her.

"Don't come near me, you hard-hearted man!" she whispered. "It's your fault that I'm to go to my death at the stake."

"I can't let that happen. I was given permission to speak to you by telling the prince that

No Challenger Appeared.

you might confess to me. But that's not what I want. Please, Rebecca, climb up on my horse with me. We will flee this combat and flee England together. I no longer care that the name of Bois-Guilbert will be shamed and dishonored. I care only that you live."

"Leave me! You are my enemy. You are evil! I'd rather die than run away with you."

Fitzurse came out onto the field and asked the Templar, "Well, has she confessed?"

"No. Take your hands off my reins or —"

But at that moment, a knight sped onto the field and stopped the Templar's protest. In spite of the crowd's desire to see a witch burned, a cry went up. "A challenger is here! Rebecca's challenger has arrived!"

But as horse and rider came closer, the exhausted appearance of the animal and the unsteady posture of the rider dismayed the crowd. However, when the knight was asked to identify himself, he spoke in a firm voice.

"I am a noble knight ready to defend Rebec-

A Knight Sped onto the Field.

ca with my sword and lance, to prove that the accusations against her are false, and to defy Brian de Bois-Guilbert, who is a traitor, a liar, and a murderer!"

"Who dares make those accusations? Your name, Sir Knight?" demanded the Templar.

Raising his helmet, the knight replied, "A name and lance you know well, Bois-Guilbert, for they defeated you in tournaments in the Holy Land and at Ashby. My name is Ivanhoe!"

With that, he closed his visor and rode toward his starting post, his lance upright. The Templar did the same, but as his squire assisted him in his final preparations, he noticed that his master's face was strangely pale and he was almost gasping for breath.

Once the two knights were in place, the trumpets blared and the charge began. Ivanhoe's weary horse went down at the first thrust of Bois-Guilbert's lance. Even though Ivanhoe's lance barely touched the Templar's

"My name is Ivanhoe!"

shield, Bois-Guilbert reeled in the saddle and fell from his horse.

Ivanhoe pulled himself free from under his fallen horse and got to his feet. Placing his sword at the bars of the Templar's visor, Ivanhoe commanded, "Give up or die!" But Bois-Guilbert didn't move.

"Wait! Don't slay him!" cried Prince John. "We acknowledge you, Ivanhoe, the winner."

John's guards rushed onto the field to aid the Templar, but when they removed his helmet, they found his eyes closed and his face ashen. Brian de Bois-Guilbert was dead.

"He didn't die from my lance," said Ivanhoe, "and I don't claim his horse or armor or weapons as my reward. His heart failed him as a punishment for his crimes."

At that moment, hundreds of horses rode onto the field, shaking the ground before them. Leading the group of knights and soldiers and yeomen was the Black Knight.

Stopping before Ivanhoe, the Black Knight

Brian de Bois-Gilbert was Dead.

cried, "Foolish lad! You shouldn't have attempted this combat while you were still so weak. But it turned out well, and you saved the maiden's life."

Then, turning to the royal gallery, the Black Knight called, "Waldemar Fitzurse, I arrest you on charges of treason."

"Who dares arrest my advisor?" demanded Prince John.

"I do," replied the Black Knight, as he removed his helmet. "I, King Richard of England, the brother you hoped was dead."

Prince John fell back into his chair. "But-but I didn't—"

"Silence, brother! In spite of your treachery, I cannot condemn you, my own flesh and blood, to death. You will stay at our mother's castle until all is quiet and there is peace between Saxons and Normans."

"Long live King Richard! Long live the Lion-Hearted!" cheered the spectators.

Isaac had arrived with King Richard and

"The Brother You Hoped Was Dead."

now rushed to his daughter's side. "Let us hurry and thank Ivanhoe this very moment."

"No, I cannot. I fear that I will show my true feelings for him, and that can never be. Ivanhoe loves Rowena and it is she who will become his wife, just as they have planned for so many years. I have no place in his life."

"As you wish, my child," said Isaac as he took his daughter in his arms and led her off the field.

Rebecca and Isaac traveled to Spain, where they lived peacefully and where Rebecca continued caring for the sick and wounded.

Cedric welcomed Ivanhoe back into his home, proud of his son's bravery and happy to approve of his marriage to Rowena.

King Richard's hopes for peace finally did come to pass, and Saxons and Normans learned to live together. As for Ivanhoe, he went on to distinguish himself in the service of King Richard for many years to come.

Happy To Approve His Marriage